I Belong

SUZANNE K. WHANG

A novella inspired by true events

Published October 2018
Copyright © 2018 Suzanne K. Whang
Cover design by Chad Bartlett
ISBN-13: 978-0-692-16121-0

Acknowledgements

To my wonderful friends, thank you for your prayers, honest feedback, and a swift kick in the behind when I wanted to give up! You're the best.

Dedication

To my Lord and Savior. And to the remarkable people on the autism spectrum who daily endure being misunderstood and mistreated—never forget that you are perfect in His eyes.

Contents

Chapter One

Seth Porter drives up to an overcrowded parking lot in his blue Honda Accord. It's move-in day for freshman at Wakesville University, and the campus is swarming with families dropping off fresh-faced kids. Seth is the only one there without anyone to help him, but that doesn't seem to bother him.

He parks his car, making sure it's perfectly aligned and evenly spaced, then gets out, scrunching his tall frame through the door. He takes one of his cardboard boxes out of the trunk and heads up the hill.

From somewhere behind him comes the soft, drawn-out cry of a bird. Seth turns around and fixes his hazel eyes on a mourning dove, perched atop a wire link fence. It cocks its head from side to side, then flies away.

Suddenly, a car horn blares. Seth realizes he's standing in the street and steps onto the sidewalk. He continues up the hill to the East Gate of the campus. An emblem affixed on top of the wrought-iron gate says, Wakesville University, *Lux et Aequalitas*. Seth remembers from his high-school Latin class that this means light and equality.

He enters through the gate and walks past manicured lawns, sloping walkways, and Gothic-style buildings. Students and parents carry boxes and furniture to and fro. Seth looks toward the football stadium and sees that it's been repaired since the tragedy that took place there less than a year ago.

He arrives at a box-like building marked "Science and Engineering Interest Dorm," a learning community for gifted students. He enters through the double doors and glances at the registration desk where two upperclassmen are sitting. A buff guy is wearing a T-shirt that reads, "Trust Me, I'm an Engineer." Next to him is a pensive looking girl with long auburn hair, loosely braided down her back. Seth doesn't realize he's supposed to stop at this desk.

"Excuse me," the girl asks. "Would you like to register and get your key?" Seth stops and looks at her with a blank stare. He studies her perfectly round eyes and pale skin.

"What's your name?" she asks.

"Uh, Seth Porter."

She hands him his welcome packet and has him register on a laptop. He forgets to thank her and heads down the hall to his room. He opens the door and looks at the furniture: two chunky dressers, two small desks, and two long beds with striped mattresses. Some clothes are already hanging in one of the closets.

Seth puts down his cardboard box on one of the tables and takes out a heavy toolbox and a plastic container full of metal parts.

Just then, a student bursts into the room carrying a TV. He's solidly built and tightly wound, like a coil ready to spring. "Hi, I'm Kwan. Your cellmate." He puts down the TV and extends his hand toward Seth.

Seth looks at his hand and barely touches it. "Nice to meet you... Komodo dragon."

"What?" asks Kwan, puzzled.

"Oh—I name people by the animal they resemble. A kind of taxonomy to help me remember them. I know the phylum, class, order, family, genus, and species of hundreds of animals."

"Why Komodo dragon? I'm not Indonesian," Kwan says.

"It's the way you walk." Seth demonstrates by plodding and swaying from side to side.

Kwan shakes his head and says, "You sure know how to make a good first impression."

Seth is confused by Kwan's cynicism. "Komodo dragons are fierce, almost indomitable."

"OK, then. I'll take that as a compliment," Kwan says.

Seth opens his plastic box and takes out several clunky metal parts. He jiggles the interlocking pieces together end to end to make something resembling a Franken-snake.

"What you got there?"

"It's a prototype of a snake-bot."

It clicks loudly as Seth fiddles with it. The auburn-haired girl at the desk peers into the room. Behind her is the other upperclassman who was at the desk with her.

"What's this?" she asks.

Seth gets nervous and launches into an animated explanation. "This is a bio-hack of a python I've been working on for the past four years. The concept is not new. Its muscular front crawl has already been replicated in snake-bots. This little camera at the end has also been achieved by a defense contractor. But I'm working on adding other capabilities."

The girl focuses her attention on the contraption. "This would be perfect for DSRD. We don't have anything to submit yet."

"I'm well aware of the Defense System R&D Competition, red panda."

"What?" she asks.

Kwan laughs. "Let me guess. Her hair reminds you of a red panda."

Seth is worried he's offended her too.

"I prefer to be called by my proper name, Genine. And this is Colin," she says.

"You know you have to be an upperclassman to enter, right?" asks Colin.

"Technically, I have enough credits to be a second-semester sophomore," says Seth.

"I think they make exceptions in cases like that, right?" Colin looks at Genine.

She responds, "As long as the student's in good standing."

"I've always been in good standing. I've never even gotten a parking ticket."

"November first is the deadline for submitting prototypes," Genine explains. "That's pretty soon."

"Admittedly, there are some problems I need to figure out," explains Seth.

"You do know it has to be a group project, right?" Colin asks.

"Uh, I don't do well in groups," Seth responds.

Genine frowns and folds her arms. "Suit yourself. But you may wish to reconsider."

Seth looks at his feet and can barely breathe in Genine's presence. Colin notices and chuckles.

Genine waits for Seth to look up. "There's no room at the lab, so we should consider setting up shop at my house," she says. "Want to take a look? That's if you want to work with us."

Seth obediently packs up his snake-bot, picks up his sketchbook, and trails Genine like a puppy. Colin brings up the rear.

✠

At an old house just off campus, Genine climbs a few stairs and opens the door to a messy living room. She pushes aside a one-man tent that's pitched near the entrance. Seth comes in and looks around at the lopsided couch, the tattered rug, and colored Christmas lights strung up along the ceiling.

Genine leads them to a cluttered table in the alcove. Seth watches as her nimble hands clear away stacks of books and coffee mugs.

"OK, let's get down to business," she says.

Seth pulls out his sketchbook and flips through pages and pages of intricate drawings. He points to a detailed schematic and explains, "I used hydraulic cylinders to mimic muscles that allow for forward propulsion. I still need to make it more efficient and minimize the size of the battery. All these drawings are already on SketchUp."

Colin weighs in, "It clearly has military applications, which they love at DSRD."

"I can see it being used for intelligence gathering too," Genine adds. "But why a snake-bot?"

"When I was in elementary school, my mom used to take me to the zoo almost every Saturday. One time, we got to the reptile house just when they were feeding a twenty-foot anaconda. I watched it swallow a live rat. It gave me nightmares for weeks."

Colin is worried. "This is more ambitious than I thought. I'm not sure how you'd convince the jury it's going to stand up to engineering due diligence."

"I've tested it. In my mind. I know it works. By the way, I'm going need a 3D printer soon—to make the casing."

"You'll have to leave that to us because only upperclassmen are allowed to use the 3D printer," Colin says.

Seth turns away and thinks to himself. *How do I know they're going to do it right? What if they ruin it?*

Colin sees how uncomfortable Seth is. "Look, you just have to trust us."

Seth doesn't respond.

‡

Seth sits at his desk in his room mumbling to himself as he draws in his sketchbook. Kwan is zoned out playing League of Legends on his computer.

A stocky, athletic floormate named Nash comes rushing into their room. Seth looks up and says, "Badger." Nash is followed by another floormate, Fergus, who's chewing on a toothpick. Seth points to him and says, "Anteater."

Fergus is a ball of nerves. "Quick, turn on the news. They're supposed to make an announcement."

Kwan grabs the remote and turns on the TV. A local news reporter speaks into a microphone. "Trevor Kendrick, who allegedly set off a bomb at Wakesville University's homecoming game last year—killing eighteen students and injuring thirty-nine people—has been deemed mentally competent to stand trial."

An inset of Trevor Kendrick's mugshot appears on the bottom of the screen. He looks angry and depressed.

Seth coughs, takes out an inhaler from his pocket, and puffs a few times.

Fergus ogles Seth. "Ever been told you look like him?"

The reporter continues. "Here with me is Dr. Owens, president of Wakesville University. Dr. Owens, what are your thoughts on this announcement?"

Dr. Owens, a silver fox with a slight double chin, leans toward the microphone and says, "Our thoughts and prayers are with the families of the victims. We want to see justice served. For their sake. We feel it's only right that Trevor Kendrick should stand trial."

"It's been almost a year since the incident. Are the authorities any closer to a motive?"

"I'm not privy to that information. We've submitted everything we have on this case. It's in their capable hands now."

"As you said before, this has been a very difficult year for the university."

"Indeed. Our community has been shaken to the core. It's going to take time to heal—to regain a sense of normalcy, if you will."

"Dr. Owens, the question on everybody's mind is—what has the university done since the tragedy to keep students safe—especially with the freshmen arriving?"

"Absolutely. As you can imagine, the safety of our students has become our top priority. I'm happy to report that, over the summer, we worked around the clock to double the number of cameras, metal detectors, and blue-light phones. We've also set up an anonymous tip line, and we're asking students to report anything suspicious." Dr. Owens looks directly into the camera. "Anything even remotely suspicious should be reported to the Office of Student Conduct. Immediately."

Fergus nods in agreement. Nash turns down the volume and whistles in disbelief. "How can Kendrick not be considered insane?"

"He's a cold-blooded psychopath," says Kwan. "Not some looney who suddenly went berserk."

"If only his housemates had turned him in," Fergus says in disgust. "For crying out loud, he was making a bomb in their basement! How could they have missed that?"

Nash frowns at Fergus. "You're obsessed with this killer, you know that?"

Seth cuts him off. "Trevor Kendrick is still under investigation, so technically he's considered innocent until proven guilty."

Fergus snaps, "What did you say?"

"In this country, you're innocent until proven guilty beyond a reasonable doubt."

"Look, I was there. I saw what happened!" Fergus chokes up.

Kwan tries to smooth things over. "It's only a matter of time before they lock him up for good."

Fergus eyes Seth and whispers, "It's always the odd ones…"

Nash looks at a poster on the wall hanging over Seth's desk. It's of an intricate and wildly colorful spiral. At the bottom reads a quote, "My fate has been that what I undertook was fully understood only after the fact."

"Hey, you into psychedelics?" Nash asks Seth.

"That's a spiral fractal, a geometric shape found in nature that branches off into infinitely smaller copies of itself. Specifically, it's a Mandelbrot set, named after the mathematician Benoit Mandelbrot. And that's his quote."

"The Math Nazi," jokes Nash.

"Mandelbrot is considered the father of fractal geometry," Seth explains.

Fergus is indignant. "You don't think we know that?"

"That is one freaking, fantastically fun factoid!" Nash laughs hysterically.

Kwan gets up and announces, "OK, dinnertime."

"Hungry, Frack?" Nash goes into another fit of laughter. "You don't mind if I call you Frack, do you?" He asks mockingly.

Seth looks down at the inhaler in his hand and slowly puts it back in his pocket.

"Hey, enough!" Kwan insists.

"Such a killjoy, Kwan," says Nash.

As they're leaving, Kwan asks Seth, "Want to join us for dinner?"

"I prefer to eat when it's less crowded." Seth turns away and goes back to drawing. Kwan shrugs and leaves.

As they walk down the hallway, Fergus says, "You have to find another roommate, dude. How do you sleep at night?"

"He reminds me of my Aspie cousin," says Kwan.

"A who?" asks Fergus.

"My cousin has Asperger's. They're like absentminded professors."

"Aren't they unstable?" Fergus asks.

Nash shakes his head. "Seth is more like a child prodigy in need of a good spanking."

"Hey, he's harmless. Leave him alone," Kwan says.

Chapter Two

Late in the evening, Seth walks into the Underground Café, a popular java joint near campus. Kwan and Fergus are sitting at a small table with some girls. Seth places his order then studies the old LP record covers that line the walls.

In the back of the café, the proprietor is pouring a large batch of coffee beans into a commercial roaster. Suddenly, a loud boom rings out through the café. Fergus jumps to his feet. Everybody stops talking and looks over at the proprietor.

"Not again!" He kicks the base of the roaster and slumps down in a chair.

Fergus is visibly shaken and trembling. Vivid memories of the bombing come back to him. A violent blast in the mid-section of the stadium. The high-pitched ringing in his ears. Everybody looking around in a daze. Plumes of choking smoke. People screaming, running into each other. Bodies lying here and there. Blood splattered everywhere.

Fergus can hardly breathe. Other students around him feel his pain. It's all too fresh in their minds too.

Kwan puts his hand on Fergus' arm. Fergus flinches and tries to say something but can't. Kwan tries to calm him down.

Seth comes over to Kwan and asks, "What's wrong with him?" Kwan turns around and tries to hush him, but Seth insists on speaking directly to Fergus. "You know it was just the coffee roaster backfiring. It doesn't sound anything like an explosion."

Kwan glares at Seth, but Seth continues. "There's no reason to get upset. Statistically, the likelihood of another mass casualty incident happening on this campus is next to nil."

"Shut up, you freak!" Fergus screams and tries to punch Seth. Kwan holds him back. Fergus pushes him away and storms out.

"Seth, couldn't you see he was upset?" Kwan asks, flabbergasted.

"I was trying to help him be rational. Emotions are the enemy of reason."

By now, everybody is staring at Seth in disbelief. Seth slowly looks around. After a moment of studying their gaping expressions, he realizes they're upset. He gets his coffee from the counter and leaves.

‡

A few days later, Kwan and Seth are sitting at their desks studying. Kwan looks at his phone and jumps up, yelling, "We're gonna be late!" Seth slowly gets up and starts to change into a tuxedo. So does Kwan, but gets agitated, trying to figure out how to put on the cummerbund. Finally, they're dressed and ready to leave the dorm.

Kwan tugs at his sleeve. "Why do they make the freshmen serve at these functions?"

"It's a long-standing tradition that dates back to the founding of the university," Seth explains.

"I know that already. Let's go."

Kwan and Seth arrive at the stately residence of the university president. Dr. Owens is looking smart in a silk bow tie and dinner jacket. With his hands held behind his back, he walks around the lawn inspecting everything set up for an elegant garden party to kick off the academic year. Small tents are pitched here and there. White folding chairs line the perimeter of the garden. Seated near a row of hedges, a string quartet warms up.

Seth and Kwan see the party planner, a thin woman in a purple dress, tiptoeing in heels across the lawn toward them. "Kwan and Seth, I take it? To the kitchen please," she says authoritatively.

Kwan and Seth go into the house and down the hall to an expansive kitchen. In front of a huge refrigerator, the chef is wrapping an ace bandage around the arm of a waiter who is wincing. The chef sees Kwan and Seth watching and says, "You don't see nothing!"

Kwan shakes his head, no. But Seth vehemently shakes his head, yes.

"What? You gonna tell?" the chef asks Seth angrily.

"No!" Seth says.

The chef motions to the counter. "Take these outside."

Kwan and Seth pick up trays of delectable hors d'oeuvres and their way back to the garden.

To Dr. Owens' delight, the string quartet starts playing Bach's Goldberg Variations. He happily greets each guest as they arrive.

Near one of the tents is Eric Santori, a popular engineering professor who's so tall he has to stoop down to talk to people. He helps himself to a flute of champagne and joins Harold Robinson, the university's chief legal counsel.

"Tell me, Harold, were you surprised to hear Trevor Kendrick will stand trial?" Professor Santori asks.

Robinson pushes his wire-rimmed glasses up his long nose and says, "No, were you?"

"I had nightmares he was going to get off by reason of insanity."

"None of us will ever sleep well again," says Robinson, taking a tiny bite of a caramelized onion tart.

"True. Thanks to Richard," says Professor Santori sarcastically, referring to the university's director of student conduct, Dr. Richard Yantis.

"Eric, you know nobody could have prevented what happened," Robinson retorts.

"Don't make excuses for him. He knew Kendrick had violent tendencies, and yet he did nothing." Professor Santori tilts back his champagne flute.

Seth sees the waiter with the hurt arm carrying a tray laden with dishes, looking like he's about to lose his balance. Seth goes over to help him, but before he reaches him, the waiter drops the tray. All the dishes cascade onto the stone walkway in a loud cacophony of breaking glass.

Everybody gasps. The string quartet stops playing.

Robinson shudders. Seeing this Professor Santori asks, "Et, tu, counsel?"

"What?"

"A touch of PTSD?"

Robinson lets out a long sigh and shifts his weight to his other leg.

Dr. Owens doesn't miss a beat. "Phew, I thought it was a reporter trying to crash the party." Everybody laughs. Crisis averted.

Dr. Owens raises his champagne flute and proposes a toast. "Here's to

Wakesville University. *Lux et Aequalitas!"*

The guests respond in unison, *"Lux et Aequalitas!"*

The waiter has disappeared, so Seth takes it upon himself to pick up the pile of broken dishes. The party planner comes over and glares at Seth, assuming he's to blame.

"It was an accident," Seth says, looking up at her.

"Well, pick it up already!" she snarls.

Kwan comes over to help Seth carry the mess back to the kitchen.

The chef and the distraught waiter greet them. "Hey, man, thanks for helping out," the chef says. He grabs a plate of mini desserts and puts it in Seth's hands.

Seth thanks the chef and turns away, saying under his breath, "Orang-utan."

"You mean Miss Party Planner, don't you?" asks Kwan.

"No, the chef. He's built like a—"

"No. She's the epitome of an orangutan. The chef is more like a rhino beetle. Look at his forearms."

They take the mini desserts and proceed to stuff their mouths like chipmunks.

✝

Students are checking their mailboxes in the lobby of the dormitory. Seth opens an envelope and unfolds a typed letter on university letterhead. He knits his eyebrows while reading it.

"I have to meet with the director of student conduct. Someone named Dr. Richard Yantis. Apparently, I made 'abusive and threatening remarks' to somebody."

"When? What exactly did you say?"

"I don't know."

"Did you offer to show a girl your fractals?" Kwan jokes.

"No, girls don't talk to me."

Kwan grabs the letter and reads it. "Yo, this is serious." He hands the letter back to Seth. "It says you can bring someone."

"Who?"

"Me!"

Seth looks at the letter again and puts it in his backpack.

✠

Seth and Kwan wait in a formal reception area just outside the corner office of the director of student conduct, Dr. Yantis, a stout man with a permanent grimace on his face.

He is absorbed in a newspaper article about Trevor Kendrick's pending trial. When he realizes it's time for his next appointment, he shouts without looking up, "Come on in."

Seth and Kwan file into his office and sit down. "I'm sure this is just a big misunderstanding," Kwan says.

Ignoring Kwan, Dr. Yantis looks up at Seth. "Mr. Porter, I presume?" He opens a manila folder. "It says here you were heard saying things of an abusive nature."

"I—I'm not sure," Seth answers.

"Multiple people heard what you said to a student at the Underground Café," Dr. Yantis explains.

"I—I assume you're referring to Fergus, in which case—I mean—my intent was to—"

"Did abusive words come out of your mouth at any given time at that café?"

"Well, logically speaking—"

Dr. Yantis grows impatient. "We're not here to split hairs. Did you, or did you not, utter words that the student perceived as being abusive?"

"I have Asperger's, so I—"

"It's a simple question."

Seeing how angry Dr. Yantis is getting, Seth shuts down. He focuses on how the man's jaw moves sideways and downward when he speaks.

"Per our code of student conduct, if your words caused somebody to feel distressed, fearful, or demeaned in any way, it is considered verbal abuse."

Kwan injects, "I was there that night, and this seems to be a case of 'he said, she said.'"

"Are you familiar with the concept of preponderance of evidence?" Dr. Yantis asks sternly.

"No, but there seems to be a preponderance of assumptions here," Kwan retorts.

"I expect you to show some respect!"

"Sir, Seth wouldn't hurt a fly," Kwan explains.

"How long have you known him?"

"What the hell does that have to do with anything?"

"Young man, you are dismissed!" Dr. Yantis yells.

Kwan leaves in a huff.

"Let me wrap this up for you, Mr. Porter. We have substantiated that you did, in fact, utter abusive words, correct? Thus, per our code of student conduct, you will be placed on probation."

Seth tries to calm himself by focusing on the diamond-shaped pattern of the carpet. "Cou—could I explain to Fergus my—?"

Dr. Yantis taps his fingers on the table and speaks in low tones. "Your blatant lack of remorse troubles me deeply."

Seth avoids looking at him and slowly gets up to leave.

"Be advised, Mr. Porter. Any future violation will result in swift disciplinary action."

As soon as Seth walks out of the building, Kwan catches up to him. "Yo, what did that jerk say?"

"British bulldog. Not tall enough to be an American bulldog," mutters Seth.

"Dude, you should call your parents."

"I have work to do."

"Seth—"

"I haven't done anything wrong."

"I have a bad feeling about this," says Kwan.

‡

In a shaded area of the main academic quad, stands a granite wall, recently erected in memory of the eighteen students killed in the bombing. Each of their names is chiseled in the cold, dark slab.

Greg Bennett, an exceedingly large campus police officer, stands near the wall. He reads the names of each student over and over again. Out of the corner of his eye, he sees Dr. Yantis coming down the walkway toward him smoking a cigarette.

"Greg, we have work to do." Dr. Yantis inhales deeply then exhales slowly. "Make sure we've covered all the bases for homecoming."

Officer Bennett waves the smoke away with his massive hand. "We're ramping up security to the max. That's all we can be expected to do."

"Look, there's a lot at stake here, Greg."

Officer Bennett bristles. "You don't think I know that? Not a day goes by when I don't think of those kids."

"Spare me the tears. For me, it's every single second of every single day!"

"OK, OK."

"Seth Porter. He lives in the Science and Engineering dorm. Keep an eye on him."

"Why?"

"Cold blooded. Capable of—I don't know what. Says he has Asperger's."

"But what's he done?"

"If it's OK with you, I'd rather not wait till he does something," Dr. Yantis takes another puff of his cigarette.

"All right. If it'll make you feel better, I'll have a talk with him."

"And what about homecoming, what have you—"

Officer Bennett cuts him off. "Richard, trust me, I've got it covered."

Dr. Yantis nods, puts out his cigarette, and walks off.

‡

Just after the sun has set, Officer Bennett waits in his cruiser outside Seth's dorm. He rolls down the window as Seth approaches. "Mr. Porter. May I have a word with you?"

Alarmed, Seth hesitantly approaches the cruiser. Officer Bennett reaches over, opens the door to the backseat, and motions for Seth to get in. "My name's Officer Bennett. Do you know why you're here?"

"To go to college and become an engineer."

"I meant here in this car."

"You told me to get in."

Officer Bennett glares at Seth. "This is no joke. I suggest you take this seriously."

Seth realizes he's misspoken again. "I have Asperger's, so I don't always get—"

"This is not about your problems. This is about something you said to a student at the Underground Café."

"I already spoke to Dr. Yantis about this."

"Smart aleck, aren't you? Take this as a stern warning. The less you see of me the better."

"Yes. I mean, no. I *don't* want to see you."

"What did you say, son?"

"I—"

"That's enough of you. Scat."

Seth quickly gets out of the cruiser and watches it pull away.

"Walrus. Officer Walrus."

‡

Seth is fidgeting in Professor Santori's robotics class. He keeps stealing glances at Genine seated a few rows away. She's wearing her hair down today, and the subtle shades of auburn and brown fascinate him.

Professor Santori jaunts over to the whiteboard and writes HUBO in large block letters. "All of you know about HUBO, the humanoid robot that won the DARPA Robotics Challenge a few years back. To the tune of $2 million in prize money. That's no chump change."

Genine catches Seth looking at her and stares back. Startled, Seth snaps his attention to his laptop.

"All the other robots walked like humans, climbed stairs like humans, opened doors like humans. Even drove an SUV—like your grandmother." Students chuckle. Professor Santori plays a video of HUBO getting out of an SUV. Instead of walking, this silver, spaceman-like robot gets down on its knees and rolls forward on wheels.

"Listen to the thunderous applause when HUBO rolls toward the stairs," says Professor Santori. "See how the torso turns around 180 degrees. Then it proceeds to climb the stairs, backwards?"

Seth interrupts loudly, "HUBO's hands have fingers that can play rock-paper-scissors." Students snicker.

A girl in the back raises her hand. Professor Santori points to her.

"Seems to me they overstepped the criterion of the competition, which was to create a humanoid robot, not just any robot that can accomplish the tasks," she argues.

"You're right. They definitely pushed the boundaries. But the judges allowed it."

Seth raises his hand this time. Professor Santori nods to him.

"The design of a human is highly inefficient. We're upright and bi-pedal. Very unstable. HUBO's design embraces bio-mimic technology. HUBO folds down for a lower center of gravity—like an animal—and rolls forward on four wheels."

Professor Santori points to the screen again. "Bet you can't do that."

"I'm trying," says Seth.

"Walk up the stairs backwards?" Professor Santori jokes.

"I—I mean—I'm trying to build a robot like that." Students laugh even harder. Embarrassed, Seth starts flipping his pen around his thumb like a whirligig. Professor Santori studies him.

"I'm sure you will. What's your name, sir?"

"Seth. Seth Porter."

Professor Santori nods and smiles.

Chapter Three

Just before the homecoming game, hundreds of students, family, and staff are gathered at the site of the granite wall for a somber memorial service. A lone bagpiper in a kilt stands at a distance playing "Going Home." The droning music reverberates throughout the academic quad.

Dressed in black, family members of the deceased sit in folding chairs in front of the wall. They are sobbing, some of them uncontrollably. Students standing behind them are also crying and leaning into each other.

Dr. Yantis stands in the back with his arms crossed, looking even more stern than usual. Seth is about twenty feet away from him behind a group of students.

Dr. Owens ceremoniously steps up to the microphone. A long moment of silence ensues. He begins in a low voice, "I thought long and hard about what I wanted to say today. Believe me, it wasn't easy." Dr. Owens' voice cracks. Another long pause. "What do you say about what happened to us, all of us just a year ago today? We never, ever thought such a tragedy could visit this campus. We never thought our lives could be so shattered, destroyed. Our dreams for the future, our hopes—dashed."

A student sobs loudly. Nobody looks to see who it is. Seth, too, is moved, but he looks emotionless and seems to be mumbling to himself. Dr. Yantis sees this from a distance and frowns.

Dr. Owens continues. "Everything was taken away for eighteen of our beloved students. And the lives of the thirty-nine injured students and faculty were rudely interrupted. Each one of us shares in their loss, their pain. Our hearts go out to their families and loved ones. And we stand in solidarity with them in our common grief. But today, I declare that we have a new hope. A new resolve to overcome, to move on. Not only to move on but to conquer the evil that was done here. We are strong. Stronger than we were a year ago. And together we're only going to get stronger. I want you to take that truth with you into every situation, each day. For your sake, for the university's sake. Most of all, for the sake of those who are not with us here today. To prove to the world that we have not been defeated."

People cry and cheer.

‡

After the memorial, students slowly make their way to the home-coming game. Lines form outside the stadium. At the front of a line is Seth, holding his sketchbook, waiting to pass through the metal detector. Kwan, Fergus, and Nash are in another line.

"Hey, come sit with us," Kwan calls out to Seth.

"OK, but I'm not planning to stay long."

Once inside the stadium, Seth follows Kwan and the others up to the bleachers. Hordes of students, alumni, and fans continue to file into the stadium. Campus police officers are everywhere. Officer Bennett spots Seth and watches him from afar.

After the singing of the national anthem and a moment of silence, the marching band files in, followed by the mascot, cheerleaders, and the players all suited up.

The two opposing sides line up, and the kicking team runs forward in perfect unison. The kicker sends the ball soaring into the air. A booming voice from the loudspeaker yells, "Look at that bird fly!" The spectators cheer.

After a series of dumb plays, the Wakesville quarterback arcs his arm back and throws a spectacular Hail Mary pass to the wide receiver in the end zone for the game's first touchdown. The crowd goes wild.

Nash reaches into his pocket for a small bottle of vodka and takes a swig. He passes it to Fergus who also takes a gulp.

Seth can't take the noise anymore and gets up to leave.

But Nash has other plans. "Whoa, Frack. Funky sketchbook. Can I see?" he asks. Seth sits back down and opens his sketchbook.

"What is it?" Nash asks, snickering.

"They're mostly random sketches. Schematics of my design for DSRD."

"This is insanely sick." Nash burps loudly.

Not noticing Nash is setting him up, Seth eagerly points to a ___. "See how the head is actually a computer?"

Nash suddenly grabs the sketchbook out of Seth's hands and tosses it to Fergus. Seth tries to take it from Fergus, but Fergus tosses it back to Nash. Thrilled by the distressed look on Seth's face, Nash does a behind-the-back toss to Fergus, who almost drops it.

Kwan notices what's going on. "Hey, stop it!" he snaps.

Fergus again pretends to give it back to Seth, but then tosses it to Nash, who holds the sketchbook in the air so Seth can't get it.

"Give it back, or I'll—" cries Seth.

"Or what? You gonna frack me?" teases Nash.

Before Kwan can put a stop to this, Seth tries to grab his notebook and inadvertently scratches Nash's arm. Enraged, Nash purposely drops the sketchbook between the bleachers. Seth watches helplessly as it flips a few times and lands amidst the litter below.

Furious, Seth flails at Nash, who screeches in an exaggeratedly high-pitched voice, "Help me, please! Help!"

Officer Bennett appears in an instant and sees Seth lunging at Nash. "What seems to be the problem?" He sees the specks of blood bubbling up on Nash's arm and comes toward Seth.

Seth panics and tries to flee, but Officer Bennett grabs him by the shoulders.

Kwan tries to intervene. "Officer, it wasn't his fault."

"Stay out of this!" Officer Bennett pushes Seth toward the exit and down a hallway.

Seth hyperventilates and squirms in pain.

"Settle down," Officer Bennett says trying to make Seth comply. But Seth struggles all the harder.

"You're resisting an officer, son." Officer Bennett grabs the back of Seth's shirt to restrain him. But Seth twists his body around and accidentally elbows Officer Bennett in the nose. Stunned, Officer Bennett blinks and holds the bridge of his nose. A few drops of blood trickle from his nostril.

Enraged, Officer Bennett pushes Seth to the ground and handcuffs him. "Any weapons?" Frisking him, he pulls out an inhaler, a phone, and a set of keys from Seth's pocket and shoves them back in. "We're going for a little ride." Officer Bennett thrusts him forward and drags him outside, then pushes him into his cruiser and drives toward the campus police station.

‡

Seth sits at a rickety table in a small room at the campus police station. Officer Bennett looms over him. "You recall the little chat we had not too long ago?"

Seth nods.

"Then you know what's coming."

"Swift disciplinary action?"

"Smart young man, you are! I'm going to have to make a phone call to the good Dr. Yantis. Oh—should I tell him about the bloody nose you gave me? I'm sure he'd be impressed."

Officer Bennett calls Dr. Yantis while watching Seth. "Bennett here. You won't believe who I have here with me. Our very own Mr. Porter. Seems he's having a bad day. Yeah, a little incident at the game. Uh-huh, another outburst. OK. I'll see to it." Officer Bennett hangs up and smiles like the Cheshire Cat. "That was swift, wouldn't you say? Follow me."

Officer Bennett escorts Seth toward the East Gate. "You'll get an email stating the terms of your suspension, how to appeal, blah, blah, blah. Remember, you're not to set foot on this campus, you hear?"

"Suspension?" Shocked to the core, Seth stands there like a zombie. *What have I done now*, he wonders to himself.

‡

Seth has nowhere to go so he walks to his car in a parking lot. After driving around aimlessly for hours, he parks on a backstreet not too far from his dorm. He takes out his cell phone and reads an email from Dr. Yantis, outlining the terms of the suspension and the appeal process.

He makes a call. "Kwan, it's me. Yeah, I got suspended. No, I can't. I'm not allowed to set foot on campus until it's resolved. Could you bring me my laptop and some clothes?"

In a short while, Kwan arrives with a backpack and gets in the car. "You got suspended for being bullied? How does that happen?"

"I'm not sure. My only option is to appeal the suspension," explains Seth.

"I knew that Yantis had it out for you. As for Nash and Fergus, I'm not done with them yet." Kwan looks at Seth staring blankly ahead. "Hey, I told you to call your parents."

"My mom wouldn't be too happy."

"What about your dad?"

Seth hesitates. "Never met him."

"You never told me that. That's gotta hurt."

"I'm sure it's hard on my mom."

"No, I meant you. Never mind. OK. Where are you gonna stay?"

"Right here."

"Maybe you could crash at Colin's."

"He's not too fond of me."

"What about Genine?"

"That wouldn't be appropriate."

"Beats being homeless. Think about it. Hey, call me, OK?"

Kwan gets out of the car and walks away.

Seth puts his seat back and stares out the window at the pale evening stars. He whispers to himself, *even though I walk through the valley of the shadow of death, I will fear no evil, for you are with me; your rod and your staff, they comfort me.*[1]

✝

In a crowded dining hall, Nash and Fergus are sitting at a round table wolfing down meatloaf and mashed potatoes when Kwan joins them. Fergus casually leans back, puts a toothpick in his mouth, and asks, "Heard the latest on Kendrick?"

---

1   Psalm 23:4 of the NIV Study Bible, Zondervan Publishing House

"What?" asks Kwan.

"They've ruled out radicalism," says Nash with his mouth full of mashed potatoes.

"So what?"

"That means they don't think he had a political agenda," explains Fergus, chewing on the toothpick. "Probably just miffed he wasn't going to graduate."

"Never mind Kendrick. Let's talk about what happened to Seth today," Kwan says.

Fergus raises his voice. "You saw what he did to Nash. It's always loners who—"

"Let me spell it out for you. He's socially challenged. That does not make him crazy or dangerous. Besides, you're the ones who should have been suspended, not him."

"He was suspended?" Even Nash looks surprised.

The toothpick falls from Fergus' mouth. Getting defensive, he says, "I'm glad he was. What did Kendrick's housemates say about him? Oh, he was so quiet. We were so shocked. Wake up! Tell me honestly, do you feel safe around people like Seth?"

Fergus stands up and addresses everybody in the dining hall. "Does anybody feel safe on this campus? Anybody?"

People are embarrassed for him and go back to eating.

Kwan eyes Fergus coldly. "You're the one who narked on Seth, wasn't it? What did you say to Yantis anyway? That he threatened you at the café? *Really?"*

Fergus is speechless.

"You little—" Kwan stands up abruptly.

Fergus runs out of the dining hall.

Nash shoves a whole dinner roll into his mouth and tries to leave, but Kwan pulls his chair in front of him. "Take your time. We're not leaving till I've made a few things clear to you."

‡

It's morning when Seth wakes up in his car, surprised he's managed to sleep at all. He decides to go to Genine's house to check on his snake-bot.

Genine is mowing her front yard with a push mower when she sees a disheveled person staring at her. She throws down the push mower and shouts, "Holy crap, you scared me!"

"I've been—" says Seth.

"Yeah, the whole campus knows. That means you're no longer in good standing and ineligible to compete. We're cooked!"

"I—I'm appealing. Once I explain I was bullied, they'll have to rescind the suspension."

"You were bullied? That's not what I heard."

"Fergus and Nash—"

"I should have known," Genine says in disbelief.

"I've already started the appeal process."

"This is a huge university. It could take forever."

"I can still work on the snake-bot until it's resolved."

"I'm not as optimistic as you are. Colin's been working on it, but we may have to push this to next year."

"Twelve months is an eternity in the tech world. Somebody else will beat me to it."

Genine goes back to mowing the lawn.

"I slept in my car last night," Seth says in a low voice.

"Don't even try, Seth. You can't stay here. Call your parents."

Seth mutters, "I came up with an improvement on the design, and I really need to work on it as soon as possible."

Genine turns around and looks at him. She sighs and puts her hands on her hips. "It better be good, because I'm already regretting this."

"I'm willing to help with chores. I'm good at yard work."

Genine and Seth go inside the house, where Colin is busy working on the snake-bot. Genine points to her lopsided couch and says, "That's where you'll sleep." Seth puts his knapsack down and hurries to the table. He sees that the snake-bot now has the casing. "When—how did you—?"

Without looking up, Colin says, "I secured time on the 3D printer late last night, and Genine got the specs from your SketchUps."

Seth still doesn't feel comfortable sharing the work but thinks better of it. "I—I thank you both."

Genine looks pleased. "OK, professor, dazzle us," she says.

"I need to—I mean, we need to make two heads," Seth explains.

"Why two heads? Why not double up on a single head?" asks Colin.

"I mean two brains on either end that interact remotely. Each covers 180 degrees, giving it 360-degree situational awareness. And you can attach various components on them for an array of capabilities."

Impressed, Genine nods her head. "I've been thinking about the circuit board," she says.

"I don't know how to make that," says Seth.

"None of us do, but..." Genine's face lights up. "We should go to the tech expo and talk some corporate rep into sponsoring us."

"The expo? That's next week," Colin notes.

"Sponsor us? How?" Seth is puzzled.

"We find a company to custom print a circuit board for us," explains Genine. "In exchange, we wear their logo at DSRD and tell everybody they helped us."

"How do you find such a company?" Seth asks.

"Watch and learn," says Genine.

Seth frowns.

‡

Seth follows Genine and Colin into a cavernous convention hall. Visitors with swag bags and bottled water meander around flashy, multimedia displays. Seth has never seen so many high-tech gadgets before. He wants to take a closer look at all of them but is overwhelmed by the sights and sounds.

A young engineer at a booth tries to engage them by launching into his rehearsed spiel about a small, tank-like contraption on the floor in front of him. "This is a reconnaissance robot used in standoff situations when it's too dangerous for human penetration. See how the user—typically a soldier or law enforcement officer—tosses it over the fence, unnoticed by the enemy?"

He points to a video of a boxy robot flying helter-skelter over a concrete wall. It lands on a patch of grass on the other side, rights itself, and rolls on wheels like a toy tank. Then it marches forward and climbs a few stairs. "It has an internal camera that streams live video back to the user."

"Like in a hostage situation?" asks Colin.

The engineer is thrilled to see that Colin is interested. "Or even a natural disaster. Think of Fukushima. This could have given them a lot of information much earlier on, without endangering human lives."

Genine asks, "Can you load it with something other than a camera?"

"As a matter of fact, yes," he says sheepishly.

Seth points out, "That's actually a downside. It could be loaded with something like tear gas or an explosive. Too risky. I wouldn't want that on my conscience."

"We have an exclusive agreement with several federal agencies. This is not something we indiscriminately sell to rogue nations."

"You have no control over it once it leaves your factory," Seth argues back.

Genine nudges Seth away from the booth. "Could you keep your comments to yourself?"

They come to another display featuring a robotic arm that swings in different directions, picking up items with its claw-like hand. An engineer plays with a gamepad to control it. "See how easy this is?" The claw closes on a rock, picks it up, and moves it. "Look ma, no hands!" Nobody laughs.

Colin asks, "Can it diffuse a bomb?"

"Yes, this system works like an extension of the operator's hands."

Seth inspects the control center of the arm. "How does the microcontroller work?"

The engineer raises an eyebrow. "Ah, but that's proprietary information."

"I'm designing a prototype of a snake-bot," says Seth excitedly. "It would be used mainly for intelligence gathering. Or archeology. A miniaturized biotech version could be used in surgery."

The engineer looks baffled.

Colin injects, "It's—uh—something we're thinking of entering in DSRD, and we're wondering if—"

Seth interrupts. "I need someone to custom print the circuit board. For free."

Genine pushes Seth out of the way. "Actually, we're looking for a sponsor who'd be nice enough to—"

Seth steps forward. "I don't want something clownishly big. It needs to be small enough to fit inside two components. One at each end."

Again, Genine nudges Seth aside again. "I apologize, sir. What we meant to say was, we would be honored if your company would consider sponsoring us to enter a prototype in DSRD."

"Sure, Chimera Tech always sponsors teams for DSRD."

"Did you say Chimera Tech?" asks Seth.

"Yes. You did notice our logo plastered everywhere here?"

"Chimera Tech delivered faulty components in that lawsuit!"

Genine steps on Seth's toes. Seth looks at her bewildered.

"That's all been resolved and behind us now," explains the engineer.

"Wasn't there a plea bargain of some sort?"

"Please excuse us," Colin says and pushes Seth to the side. "Why don't you just shoot your snake-bot in the head?"

"I can't work with an unethical company," Seth asserts.

"We're not a customer. We're asking them to do something for free. Don't you understand we need to play nice here?"

"It's a matter of principle."

"You're killing me. Just stay out of this, OK?"

Seth is too upset to speak. He leaves the convention center and heads to the parking lot. He stands by Genine's car as people walk by, glancing at him, wondering what he's doing there by himself.

Seth seethes. What did I do now that was so offensive? Human beings are so complicated, so emotional.

Finally, Genine and Colin come to the car. Silently, Genine unlocks it, and they all get in.

"Well, that was a tad stressful," Genine says as she starts the engine.

"I'm sorry. I realize what I said was socially inappropriate," says Seth mechanically.

Colin sighs. "I apologized on your behalf and got them to agree to print the circuit board in a couple of weeks. So we're still in the game. That's the good news. The bad news is your academic standing, or lack thereof."

Seth checks his phone and reads an email from the Office of Student Conduct.

"Oh, they're reviewing my appeal now."

"Do they say how long it'll take?" Genine asks.

Seth doesn't say anything for a while, then says, "I'll get a job soon so I can pay rent."

"That's not what I was implying. I'm worried about meeting the deadline for submission."

Seth ignores her and looks out the window into the distance.

‡

The next day, Genine types away on her laptop as Professor Santori announces the assignments for the next two weeks. "Remember to keep up with your lab work. Just because it's early in the semester doesn't mean you can put it off. OK, see you next week."

Students get up and start filing out.

Professor Santori packs up his things. "Hey, it occurs to me we haven't seen Mr. Porter lately." Students look at each other sideways. "What'd I miss?" he asks.

Genine comes up to Professor Santori and says, "Uh—I hate to be the one to tell you this."

"I'm all ears."

‡

Professor Santori enters the faculty lounge in the administrative building and finds Dr. Yantis getting a cup of coffee from a vending machine. "Richard, do you have a second?"

"Sure. What's on your mind?" Dr. Yantis opens the little sliding door and pulls out a tiny paper cup of sludge-black coffee.

"I just found out one of my students got suspended."

"If you'd checked your email, you would have heard it from me."

"You know Seth Porter has Asperger's."

"I can't go into specifics about students. You know that." Dr. Yantis sits down at a round table by the window.

35

Professor Santori sits across from him. "I know Seth is socially awkward, but—"

"Our code of student conduct applies to all students, Eric."

"Seth is the only freshman in my robotics class. He's truly brilliant."

"The Unabomber was brilliant."

"Did you know Ted Kaczynski unwittingly took part in a brutal stress test when he was at Harvard? That's when he started exhibiting strange behaviors and—"

"Are you implying I'm turning Seth into the next Unabomber? Let me be clear, Eric. This university will never go back to business as usual."

"You're not the only who feels guilty about what happened. But sacrificing an innocent student to the penal system is not going to make amends. Or vindicate you."

Dr. Yantis bristles. "How dare you speak to me like that. You have no idea what I'm dealing with."

"Please, Richard, trust me on this."

"Why should I? You don't trust me."

"It's not about us. It's about a student's whole future."

"The future of every single student on this campus is my responsibility. Look, we don't see eye to eye on this. I shouldn't even be talking to you about it." Dr. Yantis gets up and walks away.

‡

Professor Santori parks his car along the street and dashes toward a running path along a river where Seth is waiting for him.

"Seth! Thanks for agreeing to meet with me." Professor Santori shakes Seth's hand. "Have you heard anything?"

"No, I'm still waiting to see if they'll overturn the suspension."

As he and Professor Santori start walking along the path, a runner passes them pushing a baby in a stroller. "Under normal circumstances, they'd be more amenable to admitting they'd made a mistake," explains Professor Santori.

"What do you mean?"

"The university is still reeling from last year. That's not an excuse, but it is a factor in how decisions are made these days."

"Kwan says Dr. Yantis almost got fired for not doing anything about Trevor Kendrick."

"That's more or less true. Now he's bending over backward to prove he's tough on crime."

"But how can he assume I'm dangerous? I don't even know what I said at the Underground Café that was so threatening."

"This has escalated very quickly. The only way to de-escalate it is to go through the proper channels."

"Am I guaranteed a fair review?"

"In theory. But be prepared to take it to the next level."

"But I don't have time. The prototype is due November first."

"I wish I could guarantee all this is going to work out in your favor."

Seth looks down and kicks a pebble. An elderly couple ambles by and smiles at him. "I don't even know if I'm a good person anymore. How can I be sure when people in authority say I'm not?"

"You are a good person, Seth. And the most gifted student I've ever had. Never forget that, no matter what."

Chapter Four

Seth parks his car at a strip mall in front of a pet store called Fin & Fur. He steps in through the double doors and pauses for a moment, overwhelmed by the smell of animals. He walks around inspecting all the pets and supplies, then heads toward the manager's office. She's writing something on a piece of paper when Seth quietly walks in.

"Yikes, you scared me," she says.

"My name is Seth Porter. I'm a student at Wakesville University. Well, technically, I'm still a student but—"

"Nice to meet you. What can I do for you?"

"I noticed the parakeets aren't getting enough diffused sunlight where they are. And the ferrets aren't getting enough privacy. They should really be in the back. And there's sand in all the reptile tanks. Some species of reptiles prefer bark."

"Uh…I see you've worked at a pet store before?"

"No, but I've read a lot. I was wondering… I have to pay rent to my landlady. Actually, she's not my landlady. She's my…"

"Your girlfriend?" The manager winks.

"Not in a way that could be described as—"

"You know what? I just lost a clerk. Would you like to fill in?"

"Fill in?" Seth is confused.

"Take the place of the clerk who left. In other words, you're hired!"

"You mean to work here?"

"Yes, we have a lot to do before the holidays. Can you start right away? Jack will show you around."

Seth is too happy to speak. He stands there staring at the manager when a clerk named Jack comes in and taps him on the shoulder.

"Jack," says the manager. "Seth will be working with you. Please show him around."

Jack gestures to Seth to follow him. As they walk down the aisles, he asks Seth, "So you like animals?"

Seth nods.

"Enough to clean up after them because that's pretty much all we do around here. Scoop up poop and stuff. Wet poop, hard poop, new poop, old poop, brown poop, gray poop..."

Seth is too busy looking around to pay attention to Jack's rambling.

‡

The next day, Seth shows up to work wearing a red Fin & Fur T-shirt. A customer peers into a cage. "Excuse me, what are these?"

"Chinchillas. They're like guinea pigs, except with tails," Seth eagerly explains.

"Cute."

"Chinchillas are native to the Andes. Chile to be exact. But these were most likely raised on a farm, probably not too far from here."

"Chinchillas chillin' on a farm? That, I have to see," she laughs. "And what's this over here?"

"A leopard gecko."

"I think that's what my son wants."

"Leopard geckos originate in Pakistan and India, but this one is from a local breeder. What's interesting about him is that he's ectothermic."

"The breeder?" She laughs again.

"No, the gecko."

She sees that Seth doesn't get her jokes but finds him endearing all the same.

"They have to rely on an external heat source," Seth continues. "That's what makes them metabolically efficient. They sleep all day in the desert absorbing energy, which they use at night to hunt."

"Interesting. So how much care do they need?"

"First you need to recreate the lizard's natural habitat. An aquarium with sand, a structure for the lizard to hide under, another structure for it to crawl on..."

"Sounds like a lot of work."

"And a heat lamp with a timer to mimic the sun, a thermometer, a watering hole. And for food, you'll need a steady supply of live crickets."

"Hmmm…can you recommend something easier?"

"There are many robotic pets on the market that require no care at all."

She laughs hysterically, but Seth has no idea why.

A man with a goatee approaches him.

"You seem to know a lot," he says. What's the difference between these two frogs?"

Seth explains, "This one is an African dwarf frog, and that one is a green tree frog. That one over there is an Oriental fire-bellied toad, not a frog at all."

The woman jokes, "What size batteries do they take?" Again, Seth doesn't get it.

The customer with the goatee looks at the woman. "Oh, was he helping you?"

Seth can't tell who's talking to whom anymore and starts speaking very quickly. "You shouldn't touch a fire-bellied toad because they have toxins on their skin. It's a defense mechanism that can kill another frog in minutes."

The man asks, "The one with the red stomach?"

"Another reason why you shouldn't touch the Oriental fire-bellied toad is that the oils on your skin are harmful to the toad."

"I'm only interested in frogs," says the man.

"In general frogs are easier to take care of than lizards."

"Never mind," says the man and walks away, shaking his head.

Jack rushes by and says, "It's time to feed the snakes."

Seth heads to the aisle lined with rodents on one side and snakes on the other. He takes a deep breath, reaches into a cage, and takes out a wriggling white mouse by the tail. He reluctantly drops it into an aquarium where a corn snake is coiled up in the corner. The snake immediately takes an interest, slowly slithers over, and strikes the little mouse with lightning speed.

Seth watches the snake unlock its jaw impossibly wide and suck the mouse into its mouth. The mouse's naked tail continues to twitch as the body undulates down the snake's gullet. Seth feels the blood drain from his head.

‡

Seth returns to Genine's house and almost walks into the one-man tent in the doorway, where Genine is lying inside, talking on the phone. He goes to the kitchen and puts away some groceries then takes a can of bamboo shoots to Genine.

"I got paid so I can pay rent now." Seth sees her on her back with her bare legs crossed in the air. He quickly looks away.

"Red pandas are herbivores, like you," he says with his head turned. "So I got you some bamboo shoots."

Genine zips up the tent.

Seth is taken aback. He goes to the kitchen and throws away the can, then goes over to the table to work on the snake-bot.

‡

It's a busy Saturday morning at Fin & Fur. Music is playing, and customers and milling about. A small boy stands in front of a tank full of neon-colored fish. He sees Seth and tugs on his shirt. "How do they glow like that?" he asks.

"A group of scientists set out to create a genetically modified fish that could detect pollution by fluorescing whenever they encounter environmental toxins."

The boy looks up at Seth, dazed.

"Then these scientists patented the fluorescent fish," Seth continues.

"What do they look like at night?" the little boy asks.

Not hearing the question, Seth says, "They're the first genetically modified animals to be sold commercially."

The boy looks puzzled. "What's your name?"

"Tetra. They're called Tetra, and they come in different colors. Popping blue, lightning green, firecracker pink, star-spangled red, and blazing orange."

Jack runs by in a panic. "Seth! Quick, help me clean up." Jack hands Seth a mop and bucket and points to a spill at the end of the aisle.

Seth dutifully mops up the puddle. But as he's carrying the bucket to the back room, the mop handle hits one of the track lights, shattering the bulb. Alarmed, Seth loses his balance and drops the bucket. Dirty water spills everywhere. Customers move away, disgusted.

The manager rushes over. "We'll have this cleaned up in a jiffy."

Seth gets down on his knees, frantically trying to wipe up the mess with his bare hands.

"Seth, go get a dry mop," the manager says.

Jack rushes over. "It's OK. I got it!"

Seth is losing it. He slaps his head with his dirty hands as customers stare. The manager is flabbergasted. "Seth, Seth! Get a grip on yourself!"

Jack pulls him up and says, "Dude, calm down!"

Seth pushes him away and stumbles away, bumping into the aisles and knocking things over.

☩

Seth walks into Genine's house looking dirty and despondent. He tries to work on the snake-bot but can't. He slumps down on the couch and looks at the floor.

Genine comes out of her room. "What's up?"

"I'll get another job."

Genine sees how upset Seth is and guesses correctly that he was fired. "No worries. Just make me a majority shareholder in your company."

"A what?"

"Stocks. You know, when your slither-bot company goes public."

Seth gives her a blank look.

"Did I just stumble on something Professor Porter is not an expert in?"

"There are many things that are a complete mystery to me." Seth's lips tremble.

Genine sits down next to him. "Like?"

"People."

"Humanoids?" Genine jokes, trying to cheer him up.

"It's not lost on me that this is why I'm in so much trouble. Clearly, logic is not enough to get by in this world."

"Maybe people are just jealous of your massive brain cells."

"No, they don't like me because I'm odd. That's why I was bullied for most of my life."

"Really? How?"

"Oh, the usual pushing and name calling. When I was young, I had a habit of drawing on my arm when I couldn't find any paper. A teacher made me stand in front of the whole class and show everybody my arm. She said I was practicing to become a famous tattoo artist. That got a good laugh."

"A teacher did that?" asks Genine.

"Yeah. High school was the worst. My classmates made a Facebook page where they posted photos of me, taken without my knowledge, and ran caption contests."

"What did you do?"

"Just avoided everybody. Somehow, I thought college would be different."

"You'd think it would be."

"I'm beginning to wonder if there's something terribly wrong with me." Seth looks at Genine, making her feel uncomfortable. She abruptly gets up and goes to the kitchen.

Seth looks down at the floor again, then forces himself to get up. "Time's running out. I can't wait around for them to make a decision. I have to talk to Dr. Yantis—make him see I'm a safe person."

"That may not be a good idea," Genine warns. But Seth doesn't listen.

‡

Seth walks toward the campus and enters the gymnasium where there's a pre-season wrestling tournament going on. It's loud and chaotic as hordes of wrestlers from multiple teams square off against each other on mats laid out all over the gym. Seth scans the bleachers and finds Dr. Yantis sitting in the middle row.

Dr. Yantis sees him approaching and narrows his eyes. "What are you doing here?"

"I called your receptionist. She said you were unavailable because you were at a sporting event. This is the only one going on today, so I—"

"You're not even supposed to be on campus."

"Technically, this is not on the main campus, so I'm not in violation of the terms of the suspension. I...I really need to talk to you."

"This is neither the time nor the place." Dr. Yantis goes back to watching a match where two wrestlers are circling each other like panthers.

Seth is determined. "I—I'm working on a prototype for the Defense Systems R&D competition, and it requires participants to be in good academic standing."

"I guess that disqualifies you, doesn't it?" Dr. Yantis smirks.

"But I was bullied. You were probably not informed of the circumstances leading up to—"

"That's what the appeal process is for. You just have to wait for the outcome."

"But the deadline for presenting the prototype is November first, and the team can't do it without me."

"You should have thought of that before you did what you did."

The match is heating up, and Dr. Yantis wants to put an end to the conversation. "Let me be clear. There are always consequences to poor decisions."

"But I'm not a dangerous person."

"There you go again, showing a distinct lack of remorse." Dr. Yantis returns his focus to the match.

A wrestler takes a shot by lunging forward and wrapping his arms around his opponent's leg, taking him down with a humiliating thud. In one continuous motion, the wrestler gets on top of his opponent's chest. The opponent turns red and arches his back high, desperately rolling his shoulders left and right.

The crowd goes wild. The ref drops to his stomach and sees that both shoulders are now touching the mat. He starts counting. One, two, three! He slaps the mat and blows the whistle, declaring a pin. The crowd jumps up and down cheering.

Seth sees how slowly the defeated wrestler gets back up and hangs his head, while the ref takes the wrist of his victor and raises it in the air. Dr. Yantis bellows at the top of his lungs. Seth studies his jaw—how it almost unhinges and moves unnaturally far to one side, then down.

When the excitement subsides, Dr. Yantis collects himself and sees Seth staring at him. "Why are you still here?"

Seth quietly gets up and leaves. Deep in thought, he walks through the lobby of the gym, past a cluster of people eating soft pretzels. Once outside, he walks slowly, then picks up speed. Faster and faster, sprinting down the street, around the corner, down another street, all the way back to Genine's house.

He rushes in, panting, and goes to work on the snake-bot again. Genine and Colin are heating up some soup. "Want some?" asks Genine.

Seth doesn't hear. "What if the jaw could move a few notches to the side, rotate 180 degrees, and line up with the top of the head? Now it's a tool—a prong or a probe." Seth demonstrates with his hands in pantomime. "On a larger model with more power it could be a spade or a ram," he explains.

"The more capabilities it packs, the more points we'll get," says Colin.

"I take it HUBO's rotating torso was your inspiration?" asks Genine.

"Actually, Dr. Yantis' mandible. He has an uncanny ability to unlock his jaw and move it to the side, then down, almost like an herbivorous dinosaur."

"Rumor has it an irate student punched him in the jaw," says Colin. "He had to have it wired shut for a while."

"He is rather stout, like an Ankylosaurus. I should change his taxonomic species to Ankylosaurs instead of British bulldog."

Genine sees the soup boiling over and runs to the stove. She ladles the soup into bowls. Seth continues working, mumbling to himself.

"Blink once if you want soup after all," calls out Genine.

Seth shakes his head.

"You don't eat, you don't sleep. All you do is work," says Genine.

"Did Chimera Tech say when they'd be done?" Seth asks.

"Soon. That gives us a nanosecond to kick back and relax. Seth, have you ever been to a party?"

Seth shakes his head. Genine smiles slyly. "Want to join us?"

‡

Seth, Genine, and Colin approach the steps of a fraternity house. Genine sees a friend of hers and calls her over. "Alexis, this is my cousin, Seth."

"Genine didn't tell me her cousin was so cute," Alexis smiles flirtatiously at Seth.

"I'm not her cousin," Seth says adamantly.

"How do you know her then?"

"I live at her house," Seth answers.

Alexis raises her eyebrow at Genine. "You never told me that!"

"No, no, it's nothing like that," Genine explains.

They enter the house where a raucous party is in full swing—loud music, sweaty people, kegs of beer on the floor. Seth grimaces. Genine and Alexis waste no time getting beer for themselves.

Seth stands in the corner, looking at everybody getting plastered. Every once in a while, he looks at his watch and taps his foot.

Alexis comes over to him, holding a plastic cup of mostly beer foam. "What's the matter, Seth?"

"Getting so drunk as to make one's eyes protrude like a Boophis frog is not my idea of a productive evening," he sulks.

Alexis stands very near him and whispers in his ear, "If I kiss you, will you turn into a knight in shining armor?"

"The frog turns into a prince in the Grimm's fairy tale, not a knight."

Alexis giggles and kisses him on the cheek then waits for him to return her kiss. When he doesn't, she frowns and says, "You need to treat girls better than that, or you'll never get to spawn."

Seth abruptly walks away from Alexis to go find Genine, but she's dancing with Colin. He can't stand the noise anymore, so he goes outside and sits on the steps. A tipsy guy stumbles into him, almost tumbling down the stairs.

After what seems like an eternity, Genine emerges, followed by Alexis and Colin.

"I'm dipping," Alexis slurs and stumbles away.

"She seemed to think you were cute," Genine says.

"She smelled like gazpacho soup."

"Gazpacho soup?"

"Rancid gazpacho soup." Seth crinkles his nose.

Genine laughs heartily and loops her arm through his, and the three of them walk back home.

Chapter Five

Late in the afternoon the next day, Seth takes a break from working on the bot and decides to make himself useful by cutting Genine's overgrown lawn. He goes outside and uses the push mower to cut a large spiral shape in the grass. Then he mows smaller spirals that shoot off the main one.

Genine comes out holding a cup of coffee and looks at what Seth is doing. She clears her throat to get his attention.

Seth looks up and says, "I'm working on a fractal design. See? But grass is a difficult medium."

"A fractal?"

"Geometric shapes in nature that split off and copy themselves infinitely."

"I know what they are, but why?"

"I want to help with yard work."

A neighbor out walking his dog passes by with his Chihuahua. It gingerly squats on the edge of the fractal shape and takes a good long pee, then shakes like it's having a seizure. Genine doubles over laughing.

Suddenly, Colin comes running out. "Get in here!"

Genine and Seth run in after Colin and freeze in front of the TV.

A reporter nervously says, "It's all too familiar a scene—police responding to an active shooter situation at a university. A student inside called 911 not too long ago."

"Oh, my God!" Genine cries. "I have friends who go there."

The reporter continues, "The police haven't released any information or confirmed any casualties. Nor are they ruling out the possibility of a hostage situation."

In the university gym, Dr. Yantis is running on a treadmill watching the same scene unfold on a TV monitor.

The reporter touches her earpiece and says, "The police have now confirmed at least one casualty. The identity of the victim has not yet been released."

Dr. Yantis gets off the treadmill, takes out his cell phone, and calls Officer Bennett. "Greg, you know what this means. Yeah, the board of trustees meeting next week. We need to show them we're doing all we can. Keep your men out there round the clock, you hear?" He hangs up and starts typing an email to Seth on his phone.

‡

Later that evening, Seth checks his email and reads: "This is to inform you that, based on your recent behavior and unwillingness to accept responsibility for your actions, you appeal has been denied."

Seth grabs his keys and heads out. Dr. Yantis is making an irrational decision. If I can just talk to him and convince him I'm not a threat, he'll have to reconsider.

Seth parks his car down the street from a large house on the outskirts of campus. He walks up to the front door and knocks. Mrs. Yantis opens the door and is taken aback to see a stranger. "Yes, what can I do for you?"

"I need to talk to Dr. Yantis."

"What? At this hour?"

Seth yells into the house. "Dr. Yantis, I need to talk to you, please!"

"You'll have to leave," insists Mrs. Yantis. Dr. Yantis rushes to the door.

"The nerve! What are you doing here?" He turns and whispers to his wife to get him his gun and to call the police.

"You can't suspend me. I haven't—"

"I'll have none of your impudence! How dare you show up at my house like this!" Dr. Yantis tries to shut the door, but Seth puts his leg in the doorway.

"I need you to know I'm not a threat. You have to see that—"

"Don't you realize I could have you arrested for trespassing?"

"Your house is technically not on the campus proper, so—"

"This is the last straw! I'm going to see to it you're expelled." Dr. Yantis starts to close the door.

"No! Please, don't!" Seth shouts. Dr. Yantis again tries to shut the door, but Seth pushes into it, causing Dr. Yantis to fall backward on the floor.

Seeing him struggling to get back up, Seth turns around and runs down the walkway, into the street toward his car.

Mrs. Yantis appears behind her husband holding a Glock. "The police are on their way," she says. Dr. Yantis takes the gun from her and runs out of the house after Seth.

"Hold still!" yells Dr. Yantis.

Seth stops and turns around. It's dark, but he can see that Dr. Yantis is aiming a gun at him. He panics and tries to run to his car.

"I said, hold still!" Dr. Yantis screams.

Seth freezes. His heart is pounding in his chest. He stands there not knowing what to do when he sees headlights approaching. Dr. Yantis quickly puts the gun behind his back.

It's a campus police cruiser. It stops just behind Seth, and an officer emerges. "What seems to be the problem?" he asks Dr. Yantis.

Dr. Yantis shouts, "This student is threatening me! Have Officer Bennett deal with him immediately." He makes sure the officer can't see the gun behind his back.

The officer handcuffs Seth and takes him away.

‡

Seth is brought into a small room at the campus police station where Officer Bennett is waiting for him. "Well, well, well, Mr. Porter. When we first met, you told me you didn't want to see me none. Yet here you are again. I'm beginning to think you like me."

"This is a nightmare," Seth mutters.

"Yours or mine?" Officer Bennett motions for Seth to sit down on a metal chair. Then he pulls out a pack of gum. "Wanna piece?" Without looking at Seth, he puts a piece in his own mouth.

Footsteps approach. A middle-aged woman comes into the room holding a notebook. "Seth Porter, is that right?" she asks quietly.

Seth looks down and twists his handcuffed hands.

"Could you remove those?" the counselor asks. Officer Bennett comes over and takes them off then leaves the room.

"I'm the university counselor, and I need to ask you a few questions.

"Psychological counseling?" Seth asks, confused.

"Not exactly. Just a few questions for you. Uh, I understand you were…upset today?"

"You mean at Dr. Yantis' house, or on the way here, or…"

"I mean upon hearing about the outcome of your appeal and at Dr. Yantis' house."

"I was determined to speak to Dr. Yantis if that counts as being upset."

"Have you ever felt like you were no longer in control of your emotions?"

"Which emotions? I have Asperger's, so—"

"Have you ever had uncontrollable thoughts of harming yourself or others?"

"Not until you asked me."

"You just had these thoughts?"

"When you asked me just now, yes."

"Could you describe them?"

"Which? Anger, wanting to harm myself, or—"

"Both. Yeah, I mean, harming yourself. And others…"

"People who want to harm themselves usually write a letter about social injustice or the emptiness of life, then shoot themselves, often in the head."

"Un-huh." She writes this down in her notebook.

"In mass murders, perpetrators first kill their family or romantic liaisons, then random strangers, and finally themselves. This usually takes place in public places using a semi-automatic assault weapon."

"Have you ever thought of—"

"I'm thinking about it right now.

"Could you elaborate?"

"Perpetrators probably reason that it's more attention-getting to commit murder-suicide in one sequential act. Although they are often apprehended before executing their plan in full."

"I see. And how do you feel now?

"The same as usual."

"OK, that's all. Thank you." The counselor gets up and leaves, shutting the door behind her. She approaches Officer Bennett. "He seems to know a lot about murder-suicide. It's probably just his Asperger's."

"You don't sound convinced."

"Convinced he's not a threat?"

"That's why I called you here, isn't it?"

"You know how difficult it is to predict violent behavior." She gets defensive.

"Is he safe, is all I need to know."

"I can't make that determination about anybody."

"Thought so. Then Legal will have to make that call. Let me get Harold over here."

Seth continues to wait in the small room. He puts his forehead on the table and looks down at the floor. He sees black scuff marks on the tiles and pulls his feet away. He wonders to himself, *do they think I'm capable of harming someone? Am I? If cornered into a desperate situation, how would I react?* The more he thinks about it the more confused he becomes.

Suddenly, Officer Bennett bursts into the room, followed by Robinson, who speaks to Seth in an unnecessarily loud voice. "So, Officer Bennett tells me you're having a bad day."

"I was fine until—I mean—"

"I talked to Dr. Yantis not too long after you left his house," Robinson says. Let me explain something to you. In short, this is not good. Based on your previous behavior and what you did today, we're going to have to file for an Involuntary Admission for Treatment."

"What?" Seth exclaims.

"We need to determine if you're a potential threat to self or others. The university requires it in situations where—"

"But I'm not—"

"It's a precautionary measure. You have nothing to worry about if, as you say, you're not a threat." He clasps his hands then takes his leave.

"Off you go to the hospital," says Officer Bennett approaching Seth.

"What?"

"You heard Mr. Robinson. You're going to the hospital."

"But I'm not ill."

"I'm afraid you don't have a choice," he says looming over Seth, causing him to panic again. Seth jumps up and tries to dash out. Officer Bennett blocks his way. Reflexively, Seth kicks him in the shin. Officer Bennett sucks in his breath and shoves Seth to his knees, twisting his arms back, and handcuffing him again. "Hard to keep this pup on the porch!"

"No!" screams Seth as he's being led outside to the parking lot.

Officer Bennett pushes Seth head first into the cruiser and slams the door. He gets into the driver's seat and says, "Make yourself comfy. It's going to be a bumpy ride."

Seth squirms in pain from being handcuffed behind his back. "Where are taking me?"

"I already told you. To the hospital."

"But I'm not ill."

"Let's see what the nice people at the psychiatric hospital have to say about that."

"Psychiatric hospital?"

"Not the sharpest tool in the shed, are you?"

They drive on in silence.

The cruiser arrives at a prison-like facility surrounded by a tall fence, topped with barbed wire. Seth looks out the window in horror.

Officer Bennett escorts him to the front desk, takes off his handcuffs, and hands him over to the intake nurse. She quickly goes through a standard set of questions including, "Are you currently contemplating suicide or murder?" and, "Have you taken any psychedelic drugs in the past twenty-four hours?"

Then she makes him surrender all his belongings and hands him off to an orderly, who takes him to a small room that only has a bed in it. The door has no lock, only a wire mesh window that nurses on duty frequently peer through to check on patients. Seth sits down on the bed and stares at the wall, too shocked to think.

‡

The next morning, Seth wakes up in the bed in the same clothes.

He doesn't remember how he managed to fall asleep. He gets up and schleps down the harshly lit hallway. He glances into a room and sees a patient with his mouth open staring off into space. He walks past the nurses' station. Behind the counter, a short nurse looks at him quizzically. "Excuse me, Mr. Porter. Did you want to call somebody? Maybe your parents?"

"No, thank you." Seth walks away. Then he comes back. "Actually, I would like to make a call."

The nurse puts the landline on top of the counter. Seth dials Genine's number.

"Genine? They put me in a hospital. Yes, the state mental hospital. I don't know. I think I need to stay here for three days. Did Colin get the circuit board? Oh, I had a bad feeling about that." Seth hangs his head and slowly hangs up.

He plods to the end of the hallway and looks out the window at the enclosed courtyard. He counts the benches and shrubs and sighs. Without meaning to, he bangs his forehead on the window with a loud thud. A startled mourning dove in the courtyard flutters away through the light wash. Seth mutters to himself, *oh, that I had the wings of a dove! I would fly away and be at rest...*[2]

‡

In an antiseptic dining hall, Seth waits in line for lunch with other patients. Reluctantly, he takes a plate with two hot dogs, limp iceberg lettuce, watery applesauce, and red Jell-O cubes. As he heads toward a table with his tray, he bumps into a male patient, accidentally spilling some applesauce on him. "What the—" The patient glares at Seth.

Not noticing he's enraged, Seth casually bends down to pick up a few Jell-O cubes that fell off his plate. The man suddenly takes a cup of juice and pours it on Seth's head. Seth loses his balance and falls to the floor, splattering the rest of his food everywhere. The man reaches down and

---

2   Psalm 55:6 of the NIV Study Bible, Zondervan Publishing House

55

grabs him by the neck. Seth tries to scream. Seeing this, an orderly runs over and drags the man out of the room.

Seth sits there gasping for breath. Everybody in the cafeteria nonchalantly goes back to eating.

Having lost his appetite, Seth decides to take a shower to wash off the sticky juice. Per hospital rules, an orderly stands outside the bathroom door. There's nothing in the shower stall. No soap. No shampoo. Seth lets the lukewarm water run over his face and tries not to think.

Back in his room, he sits on the bed—hungry and cold. He thinks of the night before he left for college—his mom hugging him and explaining why she wouldn't be able to help him move in because she had to work. He remembers telling her he understood how hard she worked and that he'd be home for Thanksgiving. He balls up in the fetal position and tries not to cry.

‡

Dr. Yantis and Robinson walk down a long hallway of the administrative building.

"Harold, about Seth Porter," Dr. Yantis says.

"He's right where you want him. For now," says Robinson.

"About him showing up at my house like that. Isn't that a blatant violation of the terms of his suspension?" Dr. Yantis asks.

"You have to define on what grounds."

"For starters, he's not supposed to be on campus."

"Your house is not on the campus proper."

"He scared the living daylights out of my wife and pushed me over. More proof that he poses a serious threat. Isn't that enough to expel him?"

"Well, much of it is your prerogative as director of student conduct."

"Indeed, it is. I say we move in that direction," Dr. Yantis says looking smug.

‡

In a stark meeting room at the hospital, Seth sits at a small table with

Robinson and a rail-thin woman who is the state mental hospital administrator.

"You've been here for the requisite seventy-two hours," she says to
Seth in a matter-of-fact way. "And you do not meet the state's criteria
for psychosis, so you will be discharged at the close of this meeting,"

"I object," declares Robinson. "He continues to exhibit overtly threatening behavior."

She argues back, "As far as we're concerned, he is not a danger to
self or others."

"Three days ago he showed up at the house of a university administrator and pushed him over. He also stated to a counselor that it would
be more efficient to commit murder-suicide in a single act."

The hospital administrator shakes her head and says, "Please leave
the psychiatry to us. There's no medical reason to detain him, so he's
free to go."

"So be it," Robinson says. "But for the record, this was your decision, not mine." Then he points his chin toward Seth and says, "Mr.
Porter, based on your repeated display of threatening behavior and lack
of remorse, your suspension will be extended for the remainder of the
academic year. In addition, your case will be reviewed for permanent
expulsion. Needless to say, you will not be allowed on campus unless
we summon you."

The hospital administrator is perturbed. "Really? On what grounds?"

"Please leave the educating to us," retorts Robinson.

The hospital administrator looks disgusted at Robinson. She turns to
Seth and says, "Mr. Porter, if you need anything from social services,
please don't hesitate to contact this person." She hands Seth a trifold
brochure with a business card stapled to it, then takes her leave. Without
looking at it, Seth stuffs it in his pocket.

Robinson turns to Seth, "Do you realize how close you are to being
expelled? You're not getting your tuition money reimbursed either."

"But I worked for years to save up."

"Well then, here are your options." Robinson lowers his voice to a
whisper. "You can risk getting expelled or withdraw altogether. That
way the suspension won't go on your record. That's what I would do."

"But I've studied hard all my life to become an engineer."

"Never mind then. Have it your way. We never had this conversation." Robinson hands Seth a document and a pen. "Here are the revised terms of your suspension."

Seth looks through the document and tries to make sense of it.

Robinson says, "It's just a standard doc."

Seth blindly signs at the bottom.

Robinson takes the paper and hurries out.

In the lobby area of the psychiatric hospital, a receptionist processes more paperwork while Seth waits. She hands him his belongings in a plastic drawstring bag. Seth puts his wallet in his pocket, his watch on his wrist, and tosses the inhaler in a metal trash can. He checks his cell phone and sees that the battery is dead. He walks out of the hospital, toward a bus stop.

✝

Seth boards a practically empty bus and stares out the window as it cruises down the street. At a stop near campus, he gets off and walks toward Genine's house. The sun is setting, and it's cold and dreary.

Genine looks up from her book and sees him dragging into the house. "Oh, my God. What did they do to you?"

Seth slumps down on the sofa and starts shivering. "Did Chimera Tech make the chip?"

"There's been a delay. Colin even went over there and—"

"Tell him to go there again."

"Tell him what?" Colin comes out of Genine's bedroom without a shirt on.

Seth looks at him, then at Genine, then back at Colin again. Nobody says anything.

It takes a while for Seth to realize what's going on. He starts packing up his backpack and heads for the door, but Genine comes after him. "I thought you knew. Wasn't it obvious?"

"As usual, I failed to notice."

"Actually, you couldn't have known. This is…new. I mean…" Genine puts her hand on top of her head. "You can still stay here, you know."

58

Seth shakes his head and walks away.

He heads to his car in the parking lot. It's drizzling, so he decides to drive a few miles to an underpass near the highway. *Hopefully, nobody will see me parked here*, he thinks to himself, watching the rain fall on the asphalt turning it shiny.

With the long night ahead, Seth takes stock of his situation. *Being cold, hungry, broke, and homeless are only temporary, he tells himself. But the possibility of being expelled. And Genine...how could I have been so blind?*

He scrunches down and covers his face with his hands. *Going back home is out of the question. No matter what, I cannot disappoint mom. The snake-bot...four years of work...so close to completion...so close to showing it at DSRD. Now this...*

‡

Just as the sky begins to lighten, Seth opens his eyes. He takes a deep breath and rubs the back of his head. He reaches into his pocket for the brochure from the hospital administrator, looks at the address, and turns on the ignition.

Seth drives a few miles to the Office of Social Services, parks in front of the building, and waits. It's at least two hours before the first caseworker arrives. Seth sees her opening the office door and approaches. She is so alarmed that she drops her travel mug, splattering coffee on the sidewalk.

"I'm so sorry!" says Seth, picking up the mug. "I was at the—the hospital and—"

The woman wipes her pants and sighs. "OK, just give me a minute." She opens the door and lets him in.

‡

It's almost noon when Seth emerges from the Office of Social Services. He calls Kwan and heads to the Underground Café.

"You better have some good news," says Kwan, as Seth sits down across from him.

Seth speaks very quickly. "I went to Social Services, and the caseworker found temporary housing for me and had me talk to a Legal Aid rep, who told me of a way to request an immediate hearing to overturn the suspension."

Kwan claps his hands. "Let's hear it."

‡

A few days later, Seth drives up to the East Gate. He parks his car and looks up at the university seal. *Light and equality, don't fail me now,* he thinks to himself. He waits for somebody to come escort him to the administrative building.

"Can't get enough of us, huh?"

Seth turns around and sees Officer Bennett smirking at him.

"Come along," he says and escorts Seth through the academic quad.

Outside one of the doors of the administrative building, a sign with a red arrow reads, "Board of Trustees Meeting." Dr. Owens and an elderly trustee approach the entrance. They stop speaking as Officer Bennett and Seth walk by.

The trustee leans toward Dr. Owens and says, "I see what you mean by the augmented police presence. I should say, it creates an almost... Orwellian atmosphere."

"I'm afraid this is the new norm," answers Dr. Owens. "Well, shall we?" He opens the heavy wooden door and guides the trustee into the building toward the conference room.

‡

Officer Bennett leads Seth down a dark corridor like a hangman to the gallows. They enter an austere meeting room. Officer Bennett sits with Dr. Yantis and Robinson at one end of a conference table. Seth slowly sits down at the other end.

Dr. Yantis clasps his hands and prepares to speak when a garbage truck outside the window rumbles loudly as it picks up a trash bin. It beeps sharply a few times and then sets down the trash bin with a terrific boom. Nobody speaks until the truck has driven away.

Dr. Yantis clears his throat. "Mr. Porter, please explain why you've requested this urgent hearing."

"Uh…to determine the legality of the suspension and to block a possible expulsion."

"I'm sure you recall what I explained to you the first time we met—what would happen if you violated the terms of your probation."

"Your exact words were that any future violation would result in swift disciplinary action."

"Indeed. Yet you repeatedly showed a blatant disregard for the rules, even showing up at my house."

"I…I have Asperger's Syndrome."

"That's no excuse. Many of our students have Asperger's. You don't see them here today."

Seth rubs his wrists and falls silent.

"Mr. Porter?"

After a long pause, Seth speaks. "I…I'm not a threat. Sometimes I say or do things that seem odd or even heartless. It's just part of the Asperger's."

"Are people with Asperger's known to break the law?"

"People on the autism spectrum generally do well with structure and rules."

"What about the law that says you cannot resist a police officer?"

"I told you and Officer Bennett that I had Asperger's the first time we met."

Dr. Yantis looks at his papers. "What's your point?"

"Even though you all knew, you never offered me accommodations at any point in this process. That's against university protocol and—" Seth is losing his composure.

"There's nothing in your record about—"

"At the football game, I was being bullied by students when Officer Bennett intervened. He didn't give me a chance to explain."

"What of it?"

"If you had asked them, they would have told you that…" Seth is getting more and more nervous.

"Who?"

"The Office of Disability Services would have told you—provided resources on how to deal with people with Asperger's, and that I should be offered accommodations. That police protocol—"

"I'm not following you."

"When Officer Bennett grabbed me, it hurt. A lot. And I panicked. That's typical of people on the spectrum. We—I process the world differently. I have sensory sensitivities and processing difficulties, so police have to—"

"I was just doing my job!" Officer Bennett gets defensive.

"Po—police need to follow proper protocol for dealing with people on the autism spectrum."

Dr. Yantis grows impatient. "What is your point?"

"I was discriminated against under Section 504 of the Rehabilitation Act of 1973."

Dr. Yantis and Robinson look at each other.

Seth takes a moment to regain his composure. "The Americans with Disabilities Act obligates academic institutions to provide reasonable and appropriate accommodations."

Robinson whispers something to Dr. Yantis.

"This meeting will reconvene in five minutes." Dr. Yantis motions for Robinson and Officer Bennett to follow him.

‡

It is tense in Dr. Yantis' office. "This was supposed to be an open and shut case!" he scowls.

Robinson looks at Officer Bennett. "I didn't know he disclosed his Asperger's to you."

"I don't recall." Officer Bennett rubs his chin. "Richard, you're the one who told me he had Asperger's and to keep an eye on him."

Robinson is surprised. "We certainly don't want to admit to that. That could be construed as profiling."

Dr. Yantis squints and takes a deep breath. "Harold, did we, or did we not, comply with the Americans with Disabilities Act?"

"There's some wiggle room in how the phrase 'reasonable and appropriate accommodations' is interpreted. That is to say—"

"He never asked for accommodations or contacted Disability Services that I know of," says Dr. Yantis.

"OK. That's good for us."

"I just want to know what the worst-case scenario would be."

"We might get sued. That's if his family hires a lawyer and we're found to be in violation. Then we'd be looking at paying a fine and—"

Dr. Yantis glances at his watch. "What about what he did to Greg? And me, for that matter?"

"We didn't follow proper protocol," Robinson explains.

"Isn't what he did considered assault?" Officer Bennett asks.

"Again, all that could be construed as being a direct result of—"

"I'll take my chances. I say the suspension stands," declared Dr. Yantis.

Robinson shrugs his shoulders.

‡

They all return to the conference room and take their seats.

Dr. Yantis addresses Seth. "Mr. Porter, we double checked the facts and stand by our decision to keep the suspension in place."

"But I explained—"

"I trust you're quite familiar with the code of student conduct by now?"

"But—" Seth is dejected.

"In addition to your tuition not being reimbursed, the university will not accept any credits for classes taken at another institution while you are—"

"It violates—"

"We have a duty to remove students who do not abide by the code of student conduct," Dr. Yantis looks a bit unsure of himself. "Perhaps you'd be happier elsewhere. Have you considered that?"

Seth is baffled. "I have a right to study here. What you're doing is—"

"Wrong? You want to talk about wrong?" Officer Bennett practically yells. "Resisting a police officer and inflicting bodily harm—that could have landed you in jail!"

Seth feels they're closing in on him and shuts down.

"Consider yourself lucky you haven't been expelled already." Dr.

Yantis glares at Seth. "This meeting is over!" He and Robinson take their leave.

Seth sits there in shock, unable to move.

Officer Bennett comes over and prods him to stand up. "Elvis has left the building, kid," he smirks.

Officer Bennett escorts Seth back to the East Gate. "Well, you have yourself a restful time away from here."

"I am coming back."

"When pigs fly, you will." Officer Bennett laughs and leaves.

‡

Seth leans against the wrought-iron fence and blinks. The wind whips through his hair. His eyes water. He looks down at his feet and starts pacing.

He takes out his cell phone and calls Kwan to explain what happened.

"Stay right there. I have an idea." Kwan hangs up and says with a glint in his eyes, "How's this for respect, Yantis? Oh, you so had it coming."

Kwan calls the student-run media outlet, tipping them off to a hot story unfolding at the East Gate. He grabs his jacket and marches down the hall, banging on doors to get as many people to gather at the East Gate.

Soon, Kwan and a small group of friends arrive to greet Seth. They start texting and posting photos and videos.

It's not long before Genine shows up. She hugs Seth for a long time. Seth is overwhelmed to see her and holds back tears.

A student reporter and videographer from the university's TV station arrive in a beat-up car and start filming. Speaking into the camera, the reporter says, "We're at the East Gate where, as you can see, a lot of students are congregating. I'm told something's happened to a student with Asperger's. Someone named Seth. Where's Seth?"

Students nudge Seth toward the reporter. "Seth, so sorry to meet under these circumstances. Tell us what this is about?"

"Uh—it's about Section 504 of the Rehabilitation Act of 1973 and Title II of the Americans with Disabilities Act. That is—"

Seth is drowned out by students yelling into the camera, "Come on, get over here!" and chanting, "Bring back Seth! In-clu-sion!"

More and more students arrive to join in the action. Some don't even know what's going on. They're just there for the thrill of protesting something.

Kwan quiets the crowd and calls Dr. Yantis' office. As soon as he picks up the phone, Kwan says, "With all due respect, sir, you'd better look out your window."

Dr. Yantis gets out of his chair and looks out the window toward the East Gate. He is mortified to see a large crowd of students marching around.

Dr. Yantis hurriedly makes a phone call.

"Yeah, Greg. You know about the students protesting at the East Gate? Get out there and do some crowd control. There's a trustees meeting going on, for crying out loud!" He hangs up and makes another call. "Harold, we have a situation. Get back here."

Robinson rushes in and joins Dr. Yantis at the window. "What are they doing? It's not one of those flash mobs, is it? Oh no! They're using social media."

"Of course they are," Dr. Yantis yells.

"OK. Let's assess our options."

"We don't have any options. We need to put a stop to this. Immediately. Roger's on his way there."

‡

At the trustees meeting, a large group of distinguished men and women sit around an ornate wooden conference table. Dr. Owens is surprised when Professor Santori enters the room and whispers something to him.

Dr. Owens clears his throat. "It's been brought to my attention that there's a situation I need to attend to. If you will permit me…" Dr. Owens picks up the phone on the table and calls Dr. Yantis.

Not realizing who's calling, Dr. Yantis answers, "What now?"

Dr. Owens frowns. "Richard, I hope you don't mind that I have you on speaker phone. The trustees are here with me."

"Certainly. My apologies." Dr. Yantis can hardly breathe.

"It's come to my attention that there's a situation at the East Gate."

"We have it under control, sir."

"Am I to understand a student's rights have been violated? A student with a disability?"

"I assure you, we will have it under control very soon."

"I'm sure you will, Richard. You have my full confidence."

"Thank you, sir." Richard Yantis carefully hangs up and turns to Robinson. "Quick, how do we reverse the suspension without looking like idiots?"

"You need to make a statement. Something like, 'Upon further consideration, etc.'"

"Hurry. Write it."

Dr. Yantis absentmindedly takes out a cigarette and puts it in his mouth. Robinson starts scribbling then looks up. "What are they chanting, exactly?"

"I don't want to know."

Robinson opens the window to listen.

Yantis hisses at him, "Would you please!"

‡

Officer Bennett arrives at the East Gate in a police cruiser. The students quiet down, looking worried. Just then, Seth's cell phone rings. He answers it with trepidation. "Hello? Yes, this is Seth. Dr. Yantis? You what? Oh, the suspension? Yes, I see. OK. Well, goodbye."

Seth's eyes widen. "The suspension has been rescinded." He's too surprised to move.

Hearing this, Officer Bennett freezes and blinks his eyes in disbelief.

Kwan pumps the air. "Yes!"

Everybody whoops and jumps up and down. More texting and tweeting.

Kwan makes an exaggerated gesture for Seth to walk through the East Gate. "After you, Seth."

Seth takes a timid step across the imaginary line under the East Gate and officially sets foot on campus. Several students rush forward and hoist him on their shoulders and parade him around the quad. More people come out and join in the celebration. Seth is elated but can hardly take it in. He finds Genine in the crowd and locks eyes with her. He mouths thank you to her. She smiles warmly at him.

‡

A couple of months have passed since Seth was fully reinstated. For some mysterious reason, Dr. Yantis has asked to meet with him again.

Seth's feet crunch on dry leaves as he crosses the academic quad. He feels nervous as he approaches the administrative building and hesitates for a long time before heading to Dr. Yantis' corner office. "Uh…you… wanted to see me?"

Dr. Yantis puts down the newspaper he's reading and motions for Seth to take a seat. "I'm sure you're wondering why I asked to see you today," he says.

Seth nods.

"Rest assured, you have nothing to worry about."

Seth nods again.

"Well, I see congratulations are in order!" Dr. Yantis clasps his hands together and looks down at the photo in the newspaper of Seth, Genine, and Colin being presented with ribbons and plaques at the DSRD competition.

"First place at DSRD. You make us proud."

Seth smiles weakly.

Neither of them speaks for what seems like an eternity.

"What I wanted to say—that is, why I called you here today…" Dr. Yantis is uncharacteristically at a loss for words. He takes a deep breath and clears his throat. "The reason why I wanted to see you was to say… that… I now see how all of this could have been avoided."

More awkward silence.

Dr. Yantis leans back in his chair. "That's it. That's what I wanted to get off my chest."

Seth nods and slowly gets up to leave. Then he turns around and says, "I knew you were a reasonable person. That's why I kept trying to talk to you."

Dr. Yantis looks down and says, "Thank you, Seth."

Seth leaves the academic building and is blinded by the afternoon sun. As he heads toward his dorm, from somewhere behind him, he hears the muted call of a mourning dove. He turns around and finds it perched in a pine tree scratching its head with its feet. He smiles and walks away.

Thank you for reading this book! Please consider leaving a short review. If you'd like to know about the real events that inspired this story, go to the blog section of www.SuzanneKWhang.com.

About the Author

Suzanne K. Whang first caught the writing bug in second grade when her teacher entered her scribblings in a poetry contest and told her to never stop writing. So she kept writing as her family moved from continent to continent, then throughout college in Massachusetts, and for most of her career in Washington, D.C. *I Belong* is her first book, and she plans to keep writing —just like her teacher told her to. Connect with her on Facebook, Instagram, Twitter, or at www.SuzanneKWhang.com.

Made in the USA
Middletown, DE
06 December 2019